DISNEY

MICKEY MOUSE CLUBHOUSE

THE GREAT BALLOON CHASE

Illustrated by the Disney Storybook Artists

Published by Louis Weber, C.E.O., Publications International, Ltd., 7373 North Cicero Avenue, Lincolnwood, Illinois 60712
Ground Floor, 59 Gloucester Place, London W1U 8JJ

Customer Service: 1-800-595-8484 or customer_service@pilbooks.com

www.pilbooks.com

p i kids is a registered trademark of Publications International, Ltd.

8 7 6 5 4 3 2 1

Manufactured in China.

ISBN-13: 978-1-4508-0289-5   ISBN-10: 1-4508-0289-3

pi
kids ® publications international, ltd.

ON DISNEY CHANNEL
playhouse
DISNEY

It was a beautiful day outside the Clubhouse. Mickey Mouse was enjoying the sunshine when he heard someone calling for him.

The friends finally made it back
to the Clubhouse, where Daisy
and Minnie were waiting. Goofy
told the two about his wild ride,
and about the great job his friends
had done giving him a hand.

That's what friends are for!

Mickey and Donald reached the field first. Mickey pushed the Toon Car's flag button. A bright yellow flag popped out of the trunk. It waved and waved in the wind, and it showed Goofy where to land.

Soon, the Glove Balloon—with Goofy and Pluto in its basket—landed gently on the soft, grassy field.

"What a ride!" said Goofy. "Thanks for your help, Mickey!"

"I couldn't have done it without my friends Donald and Toodles," Mickey said.

Toodles appeared with the third and final Mouseketool. It was a map.

Mickey and Donald looked at the map. Sure enough, there was an open field nearby. It was a perfect spot to land a balloon.

Mickey pointed to the spot.

Goofy saw where Mickey was pointing. "I see it, Pluto," he said. "It's an open field where we can land the Glove Balloon."

Goofy steered the Glove Balloon in the right direction.

"Pluto!" Mickey said into the bullhorn. "Pull Goofy into the Glove Balloon!"

Sure enough, the bullhorn was so loud that Pluto heard Mickey's voice.

Pluto grabbed the rope with his mouth. He pulled and he pulled. Slowly, the rope began to move. And slowly, Goofy began to move up toward the basket of the Glove Balloon.

"Now we need to find our pals a safe spot to land," Mickey said. "Oh, Toodles!"

"Pluto!" Mickey yelled. "Pull Goofy into the Glove Balloon!"

But no matter how loud Mickey yelled, Pluto couldn't hear him. The balloon was too high up in the air.

"Oh, Toodles!" Mickey called. Maybe Toodles would have something to help Mickey talk to Pluto.

Sure enough, Toodles had just the Mouseketool for the job. It was a bullhorn, perfect for making Mickey's voice louder.

"Watch out!" Donald said.

With some fancy driving, Mickey kept the Toon Car headed in the right direction.

Toodles had just the thing—a pair of binoculars.

Along the road, Mickey saw his pal Donald. Donald decided to come along to help.

"Oh, Toodles!" Mickey said. "I need a Mouseketool that will help me see where Goofy and Pluto go."

"Oh, no!" Goofy yelled. The Glove
Balloon had taken off into the air — with
Goofy hanging by his foot. "Help!"
he called.

"I'd better do something!" said
Mickey. He jumped into the Toon Car
and took off after the runaway balloon.

"Mickey, can you give me a hand?"
Goofy was getting ready to take
Pluto for a ride in the Glove Balloon,
but his foot was stuck
in the rope!